Vivaldi
and the
Invisible Orchestra

Stephen Costanza

Christy Ottaviano Books

Henry Holt and Company ❧ New York

Henry Holt and Company, LLC
Publishers since 1866
175 Fifth Avenue, New York, New York 10010
mackids.com

Henry Holt® is a registered trademark of Henry Holt and Company, LLC.
Library of Congress Cataloging-in-Publication Data
Costanza, Stephen.
Vivaldi and the invisible orchestra / by Stephen Costanza. — 1st ed.
p. cm.
"Christy Ottaviano Books."
Summary: Long ago in Venice, Italy, a young orphan named Candida copies
music each night for the orchestra of orphans who play for famed composer Vivaldi,
and her imaginings find their way into one of his concertos.
ISBN 978-0-8050-7801-5 (hc)
1. Vivaldi, Antonio, 1678–1741—Juvenile fiction. [1. Vivaldi, Antonio, 1678–1741—Fiction.
2. Composers—Fiction. 3. Orchestra—Fiction. 4. Imagination—Fiction. 5. Orphans—Fiction.
6. Venice (Italy)—History—1508–1797—Fiction. 7. Italy—History—1559–1789—Fiction.] I. Title.
PZ7.C8215Viv 2012   [E]—dc22   2011012902

First Edition—2012 / Designed by Véronique Lefèvre Sweet
The artist used pastels on Colourfix and PastelMat papers to create the illustrations for this book.
Printed in November 2011 in China by South China Printing Company Ltd.,
Dongguan City, Guangdong Province

1 3 5 7 9 10 8 6 4 2

For Tamara McElroy

In Venice of long ago, there lived a man who *daydreamed* in music.

He'd jot down his dreams in musical notes, scribbling thousands of notes in a single day. And his music *sparkled* like the canals in spring.

"Viva Vivaldi,"

the audience cheered, as the maestro
took his bows.

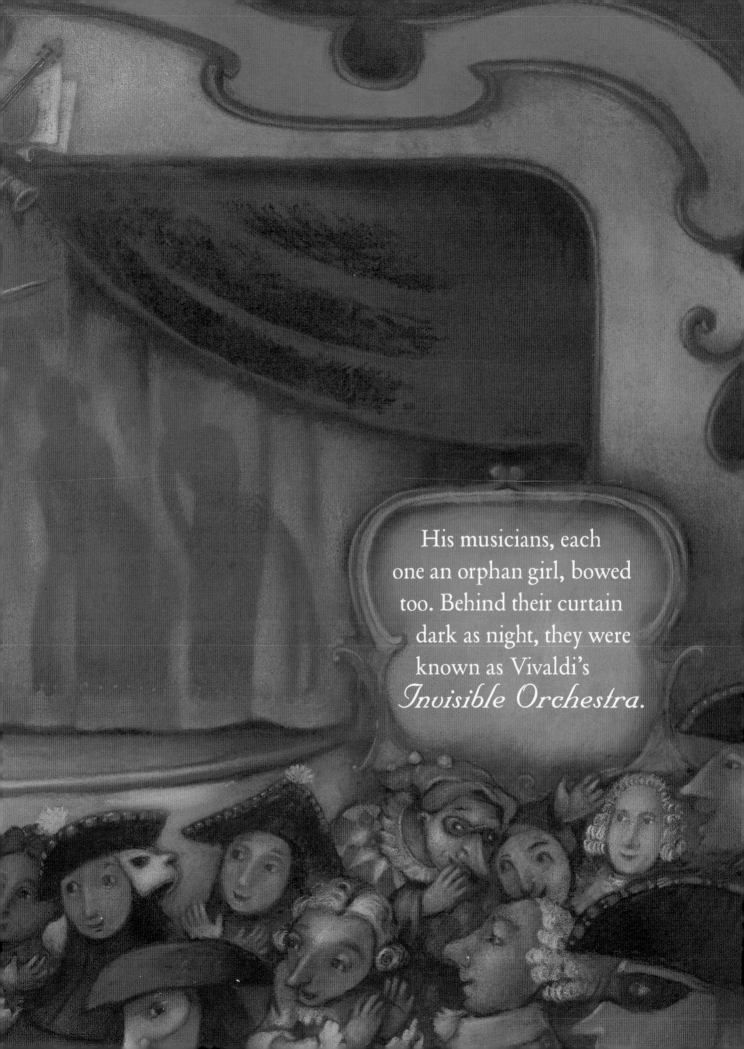

His musicians, each
one an orphan girl, bowed
too. Behind their curtain
dark as night, they were
known as Vivaldi's
Invisible Orchestra.

One orphan curtsied, twirled around, and bowed again,
although she didn't play an instrument. Her name was
Candida and, like Vivaldi, she was a bit of a *daydreamer*.

Of all the orphans who
lived at the orphanage La
Pietà, Candida had the
biggest job. She prepared
the sheet music for Vivaldi's
Invisible Orchestra.

Every morning, a *new piece of music*
awaited her in Vivaldi's study.

On one particular day, Candida read the title,
La Notte, as she carried the music up to her room.
"A concerto about the night. Why, there must be
moonlight in it!" she thought.

Her *quill* lightly touched
the blank paper, and a tiny note
appeared: an exact copy of the
concerto's first bass note.

She copied the second bass note. Then the third . . .

then another, and another . . .

. . . and before long, she had several pages
filled with *notes*, just for the bassists.

"And the violins, they must be the *glittering stars*."

She copied every violin note in the score, and soon several pages were filled with notes just for the violinists.

"The violas are the *fireflies*; the cellos below them, the *crickets*."

When all the notes
were copied and the last
drop of ink had dried, she proudly
delivered *La Notte* to the Invisible Orchestra.

First, the *bassists* . . .
"Here is your moonlight."

Then, the *violinists* . . .
"And here are your stars."

Next, the *violists* . . .
"For you, fireflies."

Finally, the *cellists* . . .
"And you, lovely crickets."

The Invisible Orchestra
never paid Candida much
attention. It was as if she
were *invisible* to them.

But when they rehearsed from the very notes she copied,
what *joy* it was to hear Vivaldi's daydreams come true!

One brisk morning, while copying notes for
a new musical piece, she thought about the title:
L'Inverno.

"A concerto about *winter*," Candida
pondered, rubbing her hands. "Why, there
must be the *north wind* in it!"

She was copying notes
in steady rhythm when a sudden
blast of frigid air rattled the window.
"And the violins sound like *frozen raindrops*!"

She imagined
herself skating on
the *frozen canals*.
"My teeth chatter with
the frozen cold," she said.

When she passed under a bridge,

it was *spring* on the other side.

The wind's *icy breath* blew open the window, awakening Candida from her daydream and scattering the music all over the room.

She quickly gathered *L'Inverno* from the floor and hurried downstairs to deliver it to the orchestra.

Between the pages of
their music, the musicians
discovered little lines of
poetry written next to
the notes.

"Birds *sing joyfully* at the appearance
of spring?" asked the violinists.

"*Thunder* shakes the heavens?" giggled the violists.

"My teeth *chatter* at the frightful cold?" laughed the bassists.

The entire room erupted in laughter as Candida fled in embarrassment.

"*Silence!*" a voice boomed.

There in the doorway stood Vivaldi. He picked a page of music off the floor.

"Birds sing joyfully at the appearance of spring?" he asked.

He tucked a fiddle beneath his chin and waved the bow like a sorcerer's wand.

There came the song of a *goldfinch*, a *turtledove*, even a *nightingale*.

"Teeth chattering with the frightful cold!" he read from another page as icy, chattering sounds flew off the strings.

The Invisible Orchestra began to improvise too,
and before long, the room was *awash in sound*.

The next day, as usual, Candida carried a new concerto to her room.

Le Quattro Stagioni read the title. "*The Four Seasons*?" she asked.

She stared at the score and discovered something entirely new: little lines of poetry alongside the notes, striking a remarkable resemblance to—her poetry! Vivaldi had created a musical landscape all to *Candida's poems*.

Later that week, as the Invisible Orchestra played, Candida recited her poems aloud. And when they finished, to great *applause*, Vivaldi parted the curtain. Candida stepped out and took a *bow*.

Author's Note

A composer can find inspiration in many things: a favorite pet, a moonlit sky, the sea. Antonio Vivaldi, for example, wrote one of his most famous pieces about the four seasons. In it we hear chirping birds, raging hailstorms, icy north winds, even a barking dog on a hot, lazy afternoon—all brought to life in Vivaldi's brilliant, enchanting score.

Perhaps not as well known are the four sonnets written about spring, summer, autumn, and winter. These sonnets, or poems, were first published with the music in 1725. To this day their author remains a mystery.

Many of Vivaldi's pieces were written especially for the young orphans at the Ospedale della Pietà in Venice, an all-girl orphanage. The forty-member orchestra performed high above the audience behind a darkened curtain, so as not to be seen, and their singing and playing made them famous all over Europe.

But what of the remaining girls at the orphanage, who numbered over 900? As a rule, they were allowed outdoors only one day a year. Their daily routine consisted of various tasks, ranging from hospice care to embroidery to egg counting. Still others were given the task of copyist.

Using a quill pen and manuscript paper, a copyist separated each part of the composer's music (violins, cellos, and so on) and copied it for that group of players, one note at a time. In this way, each player had her own page to rehearse from. Since new pieces were rehearsed and performed on a weekly basis, a copyist had to work quickly, in a neat hand, and with the greatest attention to detail.

I imagined one such orphan, her daydreams and poetry her only contact to the outside world, and Candida's story was born.